PIAZZA ESMERALDA, SAN LORENZO — NEAR VENICE, ITALY

HEY, *ALEX!* FANCY AN ICE CREAM?

NO THANKS, *TOM.* I'M ALL RIGHT.

WELL, I WANT TO GET ONE OF THOSE THINGS YOU TOLD ME ABOUT, A *"GRANADA"* OR SOMETHING...?

GRANITA. CRUSHED ICE, WITH LEMON JUICE SQUEEZED OVER IT. IT'S LIKE AN ICE CREAM AND DRINK ALL IN ONE.

COM... YOU CAN... TOO IF Y... THEM. WHEN... TO TALK IT... STARE AT... I'M A...

DUE GRANITE, PER FAVORE.

SO WILL YOU BE AT *SCHOOL* THIS TERM? YOU WERE HARDLY THERE *LAST* TERM...

OR THE ONE BEFORE, ACTUALLY.

I WAS ILL.

YEAH, RIGHT. NOBODY'S *THAT* ILL, IT'S JUST NOT POSSIBLE.

THERE'S A RUMOUR YOU'RE A *THIEF*.

WHAT?!

THAT'S WHY YOU'RE ALWAYS AWAY. *MISS BEDFORDSHIRE* SAID YOU GOT INTO TROUBLE ONCE FOR NICKING A *CRANE*! SHE THINKS YOU'RE IN *THERAPY*.

THERAPY...

EVERYONE WAS SURPRISED THEY LET YOU *COME* ON THIS TRIP, YOU'VE MISSED SO MUCH SCHOOL.

THAT'S DOWN TO *MR GREY*. MY HOUSEKEEPER, *JACK*, MADE ME TAKE *PRIVATE LESSONS* WITH HIM DURING THE HOLIDAYS TO CATCH UP.

MR GREY SAID I WAS DOING WELL, SO HE ASKED IF I WANTED TO COME...

...AND I COULDN'T TURN DOWN A TRIP TO *VENICE* AFTER *YASSEN* TOLD ME THE TRUTH ABOUT MY FATHER.

GO TO VENICE ... FIND SCORPIA ... FIND YOUR DESTINY...

SO ARE YOU—

HOLD ON!

MISS BEDFORDSHIRE! LOOK OUT!

OH!

CHEER UP, MATE.

IT'S ALL RIGHT FOR *YOU*, TOM. AT LEAST YOU'RE GOING TO SEE YOUR *BROTHER* IN *NAPLES* BEFORE GOING HOME. ALL I'M SEEING IS—

ALEX? WHAT IS IT?

THAT POSH BOAT. THERE, ON ITS SIDE...

...A *SILVER SCORPION!*

KLIK

SORRY, COMING THROUGH!

IT'S HEADING UP THE *GRAND CANAL*. BUT I'LL NEVER REACH THAT *VAPORETTO* BUS IN TIME!

ACTV

UNLESS...

'SCUSE ME, CAN I BORROW THIS?

SPLASH

MAMA MIA! IL MIO REMO!

GOOD THING THE CANAL'S AT *LOW TIDE*! GOT TO TIME THIS RIGHT...

TIME FOR ME TO SNEAK AROUND.

HMMM ... LOOKS LIKE THEY'RE PREPARING FOR SOME KIND OF *PARTY* TONIGHT.

SCUSATE, STO CERCANDO PER ... *SCORPIA?*

CHE COSA VUOLE DIRE? *VIA, VIA!*

YOU, *ENGLISH.* YOU CANNOT BE HERE. *GO AWAY.*

SORRY, I WAS *LOST.* I'LL GO...

...BUT I'LL BE *BACK.* THAT MAID NEARLY *FAINTED* WHEN I MENTIONED *SCORPIA.* THIS PLACE *MUST* BE CONNECTED SOMEHOW!

First published 2016 by Walker Books Ltd
87 Vauxhall Walk, London SE11 5HJ

2 4 6 8 10 9 7 5 3 1

Text and illustrations © 2016 Walker Books Ltd
Based on the original novel *Scorpia* © 2004
Stormbreaker Productions Ltd

Adapted by Antony Johnston
Inks by Emma Vieceli
Colours by Kate Brown
Flat colours by Nathan Ashworth

This book has been typeset in Wild Words and
Serpentine Bold

Printed in China

British Library Cataloguing in Publication Data:
a catalogue record for this book is available
from the British Library

ISBN 978-1-4063-4188-1

www.walker.co.uk

ALEX RIDER

ACTION
ADRENALINE
ADVENTURE

SCORPIA

THE GRAPHIC NOVEL

ANTHONY HOROWITZ

ANTONY JOHNSTON • EMMA VIECELI • KATE BROWN

WALKER

MAX, WAIT. A GIFT ... SOMETHING TO *REMEMBER* US BY.

AN ENGRAVED BRIEFCASE. THANK YOU, JULIA.

AND DON'T WORRY ... I HAVE NO DOUBT SCORPIA WILL BE *SAFE* IN YOUR HANDS.

OH, JULIA, YOU SHOULDN'T HAVE...

CLICK

AAAAAAAARGH!

GOODBYE, MAX.

WOW! HALF THESE PEOPLE ARE *MOVIE STARS*, HERE FOR THE *VENICE FILM FESTIVAL*. WHOEVER OWNS THIS PLACE IS *CONNECTED!*

TIME TO SLIP AWAY AND... DO *WHAT*, EXACTLY? HOW IS A *GRAND BALL* LIKE THIS CONNECTED TO MY *FATHER* BEING A KILLER?

I NEED TO FIND THE *WOMAN* FROM THE BOAT. BUT I DON'T SEE HER DOWNSTAIRS.

WE HAVE RECEIVED THE *RELEASE CERTIFICATES*, AND THE *BATCH* IS ON ITS WAY. AS I EXPLAINED, MRS ROTHMAN, TIMING IS EVERYTHING.

I UNDERSTAND, DR LIEBERMANN. THE *COLD CHAIN* CANNOT BE BROKEN. AND NOW THE BOXES WILL BE FLOWN TO ENGLAND.

THAT'S *HER!* BUT WHO'S THE *PLAGUE DOCTOR* WITH HER?

AND THE DOOR'S JAMMED TIGHT. *GREAT.*

THAT'S THE *STORM SURGE* SIREN! VENICE IS FLOODING... AND THIS ROOM WILL *FILL UP!* NILE PUT ME IN HERE TO *DROWN!*

THAT LOOSE FLOORBOARD IS MY ONLY CHANCE! IT'S AROUND *HERE* SOMEWHERE...

KKRUNCH

GOT IT! THERE'S A PIPE, AND WATER RUSHING *IN*... SO IT MUST ALSO BE THE WAY *OUT!* HOPE I CAN SQUEEZE THROUGH...

NNNF! IT'S TIGHT! AND *PITCH BLACK*, I CAN'T SEE A THING!

THE *HINGES* BROKE LOOSE! THEY MUST HAVE BEEN THERE *SO LONG*, THEY'VE RUSTED AWAY TO NOTHING!

STILL CAN'T *SEE*... LET MY BODY'S NATURAL *BOUYANCY* CARRY ME UP... LUNGS FEEL LIKE THEY'RE ON *FIRE*!

Gasp!

HUUUHHHHHH!

Pant
Pant

LOOKS LIKE EARLY MORNING. THE PARTY MUST HAVE ENDED *HOURS* AGO, AND IF I GO BACK, NILE WILL KILL ME FOR *SURE* THIS TIME.

SO WHAT DO I DO NOW?

PENDOLINO TRAIN, VENICE TO NAPLES

MIND IF I JOIN YOU?

ALEX! WHAT... HOW DID YOU GET HERE? MR GREY WAS GOING MENTAL, HE SAID YOU'D ALREADY LEFT FOR *ENGLAND*!

THAT'S WHAT I *TOLD* HIM ON THE PHONE THIS MORNING. LONG STORY.

LOOK, I NEED A *FAVOUR*. I HAD TO STEAL THESE CLOTHES, AND I'VE GOT NO *MONEY*... CAN I STAY WITH YOU AND YOUR BROTHER FOR A WHILE?

SURE, *JERRY* WON'T MIND. HERE, HAVE SOME FOOD. I BOUGHT TOO MUCH, AND YOU LOOK *STARVING*.

WHAT HAPPENED LAST NIGHT?

TOM ... I'M GOING TO TELL YOU THE TRUTH, NOW. *EVERYTHING*. BUT YOU HAVE TO PROMISE TO *BELIEVE* ME.

30 MINUTES LATER:

WELL, I SUPPOSE THAT MAKES SENSE.

REALLY? I THOUGHT YOU WOULDN'T BELIEVE ME.

WHY NOT? IT EXPLAINS ALL THOSE *DAYS OFF*, YOUR *INJURIES*, THE WAY YOU BEAT UP MIKE COOK THAT TIME WHEN HE WAS *BULLYING* ME...

BEING A SPY'S PRETTY *HEAVY*, ALEX. I'M GLAD IT'S NOT *ME*.

BUT YOU DIDN'T EXPLAIN WHY YOU WERE INTERESTED IN *SCORPIA* IN THE FIRST PLACE. AND WHY YOU WANTED TO COME TO *NAPLES*.

I ... I THINK MY *DAD* WAS INVOLVED WITH SCORPIA SOMEHOW. BUT HE *DIED* SOON AFTER I WAS BORN, AND MY UNCLE NEVER TALKED MUCH ABOUT HIM.

MRS ROTHMAN MENTIONED A COMPANY CALLED *CONSANTO*, IN AMALFI. THAT'S *NEAR* NAPLES.

BUT YOU SAID THIS GUY NILE TRIED TO *KILL* YOU JUST FOR *MENTIONING* SCORPIA. WHY RISK GOING BACK?

I KNOW, BUT... I WANT TO TAKE A LOOK, THAT'S ALL. IT FEELS LIKE IT'S *IMPORTANT*.

ALL MY PARENTS EVER DO IS *FIGHT*. NOW THEY'RE SPLITTING UP, AND FIGHTING ABOUT *THAT*, TOO.

SO I HOPE YOU FIND OUT SOMETHING *GOOD* ABOUT YOUR DAD, BECAUSE RIGHT NOW I CAN'T THINK OF *ANYTHING* GOOD ABOUT MINE.

ALEX?

CAN YOU GET ME IN?

TOM SAID YOU WANTED TO FIND OUT ABOUT **CONSANTO ENTERPRISES**. THEY'RE A BIG **PHARMACEUTICAL** COMPANY, DRUGS AND BIOLOGICAL STUFF.

THE **POPE** COULDN'T GET IN THAT PLACE. IT'S LIKE SOMETHING OUT OF A **SCI-FI FILM**, WITH FENCES AND CAMERAS AND STUFF.

MAYBE THEY'VE GOT SOMETHING TO **HIDE**.

WELL, OF **COURSE** THEY HAVE!

THESE COMPANIES COME UP WITH STUFF THAT'S WORTH A **FORTUNE**. IMAGINE HOW MUCH A CURE FOR **AIDS** WOULD BE WORTH. **BILLIONS!**

CAN YOU **TAKE** ME THERE? JUST TO CHECK IT OUT?

SURE. BUT I'M TELLING YOU NOW, ALEX, THERE'S DEFINITELY **NO** WAY **IN**.

DAMN. YOU'RE RIGHT.

**CONSANTO ENTERPRISE
AMALFI, ITALY**

THE ROOF HAS A *FIRE ESCAPE ENTRANCE*, AND ISN'T GUARDED. I COULD GET IN THAT WAY...

BUT REACHING IT WILL BE *IMPOSSIBLE*. THE FENCE IS SIX METRES HIGH, TOPPED WITH *RAZOR WIRE*... THERE'S ONLY ONE ENTRANCE, WITH CHECKPOINTS... IT'S A *FORTRESS*!

TOLD YOU. AND THEY CHECK *EVERY* CAR, IN AND OUT. ONE OF THEIR CHEMISTS WAS IN MY ENGLISH CLASSES. HE SAID IT'S LIKE *FORT KNOX*.

OOOF! ANY LATER, AND I'D HAVE BEEN *TOAST!*

THE CANOPY ... *PULLING* ME TOWARDS THE *EDGE!*

TUMP

SKRRRCH

PHEW! GOT IT!

WHAT AN *ADRENALINE RUSH!* BUT I'VE GOT TO GET INSIDE QUICKLY, BEFORE ANYONE *LOOKS UP.*

THE DOORS ARE AUTOMATIC FROM OUTSIDE, BUT THE *KEYPAD* CONTROLS THEM FROM INSIDE. I WON'T GET BACK OUT THAT WAY.

ARE THOSE *EGGS*? THEY'RE ALL EXACTLY THE SAME SIZE AND SHAPE, IT DOESN'T LOOK *NATURAL*...

WHAT ARE THEY MAKING IN HERE? *CHEMICAL WEAPONS*, PERHAPS?

YOU THERE!

WHO THE HELL ARE YOU? WHAT ARE YOU DOING HERE? THIS IS A *SECURE* AREA!

I ... I'M LOST. MY NAME'S TOM, MY *DAD* WORKS HERE.

YOUR *FATHER*, EH? WHAT'S HIS *NAME*? WHAT DEPARTMENT?

IT'S ALL RIGHT, HAROLD. *I'LL* DEAL WITH THIS.

LOOK, IF YOU JUST WANT TO SHOW ME THE *WAY OUT*, THAT'S FINE BY ME...

OH, NO... NILE!

DIDN'T YOU JUST LEAVE?

AS YOU CAN SEE, DOCTOR, THERE'S BEEN A SERIOUS *SECURITY BREAKDOWN.* MRS ROTHMAN SENT ME BACK TO DEAL WITH IT.

THIS BOY IS *ALEX RIDER.* HE'S A *SPY.*

WHAT?! WELL, WHAT ARE YOU GOING TO *DO*?

I JUST TOLD YOU. WE *CAN'T* HAVE SECURITY PROBLEMS ON THESE PREMISES...

STRAIGHT INTO THE BRAIN. LIKE I *SAID*.

SWUMP

YOU'RE THE *LAST* PERSON I EXPECTED TO SEE HERE, ALEX. MRS ROTHMAN *WILL* BE PLEASED.

YOU ... YOU'RE *NOT* GOING TO KILL ME?

NOT AT ALL.

PLEASE FORGIVE ME FOR WHAT HAPPENED AT THE *WIDOW'S PALACE.* I DIDN'T REALIZE YOU WERE JOHN RIDER'S *SON.* THAT WAS A BRILLIANT ESCAPE, BY THE WAY.

beep beep

BECAUSE I'VE JUST SET A *BOMB* THAT WILL BLOW THIS PLACE TO SMITHEREENS IN *NINETY-TWO SECONDS.*

ARE YOU *COMING?*

MRS ROTHMAN IS UP THE COAST, IN *POSITANO*, AND SHE'S *DYING* TO MEET YOU. LET'S GO.

WHY SHOULD I?

I TOLD HIM MY NAME.

IT OBVIOUSLY DIDN'T REGISTER, AND HE DIDN'T TELL ME TILL THE NEXT MORNING. I WAS SO *SHOCKED!* THE SON OF *JOHN RIDER*, IN MY HOUSE...

TELL ME, HOW DID YOU GET INTO THE CONSANTO COMPLEX?

I *BASE JUMPED* OFF THE TERRACE AT *RAVELLO.*

WONDERFUL! SIMPLY WONDERFUL.

THE PARACHUTE BELONGED TO A FRIEND OF MINE. I'VE *LOST* ALL HIS EQUIPMENT, *AND* HE'LL BE WONDERING WHERE I AM.

THEN CALL HIM TO TELL HIM YOU'RE SAFE, AND I'LL WRITE HIM A *CHEQUE.* IT'S THE LEAST I CAN DO.

WHAT'S WRONG WITH NILE'S *SKIN?*

HE SUFFERS FROM *VITILIGO,* A SKIN DISORDER THAT KILLS PIGMENT CELLS. POOR MAN, HE WAS BORN *BLACK* BUT HE'LL BE *WHITE* BY THE TIME HE DIES.

BUT THERE ARE MORE IMPORTANT THINGS TO DISCUSS. LIKE...

YOUR FATHER.

I KNEW JOHN RIDER **VERY** WELL, ALEX. YOU'RE HIS SPITTING IMAGE. IT'S ALMOST AS IF HE'S COME BACK.

I WANT TO KNOW **MORE** ABOUT HIM. AND SCORPIA. YASSEN GREGOROVICH HARDLY TOLD ME **ANYTHING**.

WAS MY FATHER AN **ASSASSIN**?

HE WAS MY **FRIEND**.

AND WHAT OF YOU, ALEX? YOU HAVE AN AMAZING REPUTATION. AND I HAVE AN **OFFER** TO MAKE YOU, SOMETHING YOU MUST PROMISE TO CONSIDER SERIOUSLY.

BUT FIRST, TELL ME WHY YOU'VE UNDERTAKEN THESE TERRIBLY DANGEROUS MISSIONS FOR MI6. WHAT DO **YOU** GET OUT OF IT?

WERE YOU PAID WELL? ARE YOU A PATRIOT? **PLEASE** DON'T SAY IT'S BECAUSE YOU'RE FOND OF ALAN BLUNT AND MRS JONES.

I DON'T UNDERSTAND. HOW DO YOU KNOW ALL THIS? **TELL ME ABOUT SCORPIA.**

SIGH
VERY WELL.

THE ORGANIZATION WAS FORMED DURING THE **COLD WAR** ... THE SECRET WAR BETWEEN THE SOVIET UNION, CHINA, AMERICA AND EUROPE.

EVERY GOVERNMENT HAD **SPIES** AND **ASSASSINS**, PREPARED TO KILL OR DIE FOR THEIR COUNTRY.

BUT THE COLD WAR **ENDED** IN THE EARLY NINETIES.

EXACTLY. SUDDENLY, THE SPIES WERE **OUT OF WORK.** SO TWELVE OF THEM **MET** IN PARIS, AND AFTER YEARS OF TRYING TO KILL ONE ANOTHER, THEY DECIDED INSTEAD TO WORK **TOGETHER** AND BECOME RICH.

WHY DOESN'T *MI6* TAKE SCORPIA DOWN?

OH, WE'RE MUCH TOO *BIG* NOW, AND THEY'VE LEFT IT TOO LATE. ANYWAY, SOMETIMES THEY MAKE USE OF US, AND PAY QUITE WELL. WE'VE LEARNED TO LIVE SIDE BY SIDE.

DON'T SHED ANY TEARS FOR *DR LIEBERMANN*, BY THE WAY. CONSANTO ENTERPRISES IS LEGITIMATE, BUT HE TOOK A *LOT* OF SECRET MONEY TO WORK ON A PROJECT CALLED *INVISIBLE SWORD*.

AND WANTED EVEN MORE. I *OVERHEARD* YOU AT THE PARTY.

OF COURSE YOU DID. WELL, THAT SORT OF GREED IS *UNPREDICTABLE*, ESPECIALLY IN A MAN WORRIED ABOUT THE CONSEQUENCES OF HIS ACTIONS. HE WAS A DANGER TO US ALL.

WHAT'S INVISIBLE SWORD?

I CAN'T TELL YOU THAT. NOT YET. BUT I WILL, EVENTUALLY, *IF* YOU CONSIDER MY OFFER.

YOU HAVE MANY SKILLS, ALEX. AND BEING SO YOUNG, YOU COULD BE USEFUL IN *MANY* DIFFERENT WAYS. I IMAGINE THAT'S WHY BLUNT HAS BEEN SO KEEN TO KEEP YOU...

BUT I CAN GIVE YOU A *WAY OUT*.

JOHN RETURNED TO ENGLAND AND MARRIED YOUR *MOTHER*, WHOM HE'D MET AT OXFORD WHILE SHE WAS STUDYING MEDICINE. SHE BECAME A *NURSE*, BUT I DON'T KNOW MUCH MORE ABOUT HER.

SHORTLY AFTER THAT, THINGS STARTED GOING WRONG. YOUR FATHER WAS IN A FIGHT IN A LONDON PUB, WITH DRUNKARDS WHO MADE REMARKS ABOUT THE FALKLANDS. JOHN STRUCK A MAN.

AND *KILLED* HIM.

JAIL FOR BRITISH SOLDIER WHO LOST HIS WAY

FOUR YEARS FOR MANSLAUGHTER, IT SAYS HERE... UNCLE IAN NEVER TOLD ME ABOUT *THIS*.

THEY RELEASED HIM AFTER A YEAR. THERE WAS A LOT OF PUBLIC SYMPATHY FOR A *WAR HERO*. BUT HIS ARMY CAREER WAS OVER, AND HE FOUND IT DIFFICULT TO GET A JOB.

BY THIS TIME, HE'D COME TO THE ATTENTION OF *OUR* PERSONNEL DEPARTMENT.

I WAS VERY **ATTRACTED** TO YOUR FATHER. WE BECAME GOOD FRIENDS. IT WAS UNFORTUNATE THAT HE WAS MARRIED.

DID MY MOTHER **KNOW** WHAT HE DID? ABOUT **YOU**?

I VERY MUCH HOPE NOT.

NOW, ALEX. I'M GOING TO TELL YOU **HOW** HE DIED. ARE YOU QUITE **SURE** YOU WANT TO CARRY ON? IT MAY UPSET YOU.

I DON'T CARE. **I WANT TO KNOW**.

ALL RIGHT.

MI6 WANTED JOHN. HE WAS ONE OF OUR BEST OPERATIVES, AND A GREAT TEACHER. THEY LAID A TRAP FOR HIM ON **MALTA**.

YASSEN WAS THERE, TOO, BUT HE ESCAPED. YOUR FATHER WASN'T SO LUCKY. WE ASSUMED WE WOULD **NEVER** SEE HIM AGAIN.

BUT THEN...

WE HAD KIDNAPPED THE *SON* OF A SENIOR BRITISH CIVIL SERVANT, TRYING TO GAIN *INFLUENCE* IN GOVERNMENT, BUT ... WELL, I WON'T GO INTO IT. SUFFICE TO SAY IT FAILED, SO WE WERE GOING TO *KILL* THE SON.

BUT THEN MI6 OFFERED US A DEAL. A STRAIGHT *SWAP*, JOHN RIDER FOR THE BOY.

clik

THE VOTE WAS CLOSE, BUT SCORPIA DECIDED TO *ACCEPT*, BECAUSE OF JOHN'S VALUE TO US.

SIX A.M., MARCH 13TH, FOURTEEN YEARS AGO. YOU WERE JUST TWO MONTHS OLD. THIS IS *ALBERT BRIDGE* IN LONDON, WHERE THE EXCHANGE WAS TO TAKE PLACE.

YOU *FILMED* IT?

WE FILM *EVERYTHING*. NOBODY TRUSTS CRIMINALS, ALEX, SO WE MUST BE ABLE TO *PROVE* THAT WE CARRY OUT OUR MISSIONS. WE USED SEVERAL HIDDEN CAMERAS.

MY *MOTHER*... IF THEY LIED TO ME ABOUT MY FATHER, MAYBE SHE *ISN'T* DEAD! SHE COULD BE *ALIVE* SOMEWHERE!

NO, ALEX. SHE REALLY *DID* DIE IN A PLANE CRASH A FEW MONTHS LATER, TRAVELLING ALONE TO FRANCE.

NOTHING CAN MAKE UP FOR WHAT'S BEEN DONE TO YOU. IF YOU WANT TO GO BACK TO SCHOOL AND FORGET ALL OF THIS, I UNDERSTAND. BUT I *ADORED* YOUR FATHER.

HE SENT ME THIS, JUST BEFORE MALTA.

My dearest Julia,
A dreary time without you. Can't wait to be at the Widow ... lace with you again.
John R.

THIS HANDWRITING COULD BE *MINE*. IT'S ALMOST *EXACTLY* THE SAME.

WELCOME BACK TO SCHOOL!

KIIYYAAIII!

THAT'S *PROFESSOR YERMALOV*. HE WAS ONE OF MY TUTORS. YOU DON'T WANT TO GET ON HIS BAD SIDE! I'VE SEEN HIM FINISH A FIGHT WITH A *SINGLE FINGER*.

LET'S GO AND SEE *MONSIEUR D'ARC*.

YOU'RE **SURE** THIS IS ALEX RIDER?

SATINT PASSED IT TO US FROM A SPY SATELLITE, AND **SMITHERS** RAN IT THROUGH A COMPUTER TO CHECK. IT'S DEFINITELY HIM.

ALEX HAS JOINED SCORPIA.

MI6 HEADQUARTERS, LIVERPOOL STREET, LOND

COULD HE HAVE BEEN TAKEN BY FORCE?

I'D LIKE TO BELIEVE SO.

BUT YOU **DON'T**.

JACK STARBRIGHT SAYS ALEX DISAPPEARED **FOUR** DAYS AGO, ON A SCHOOL TRIP TO VENICE.

WE THINK THE MAN HE'S WITH IS A **SCORPIA AGENT** CALLED NILE. AND THE SATELLITE WAS OVER **MALAGOSTO**, THEIR TRAINING GROUND.

THERE WAS ALWAYS A CHANCE YASSEN GREGOROVICH *SPOKE* TO ALEX BEFORE HE DIED. ALEX *DENIED* IT WHEN ASKED, BUT I COULD TELL SOMETHING WAS *WRONG...*

I THINK YASSEN TOLD HIM ABOUT *JOHN RIDER...*

...AND THEREFORE ABOUT *ALBERT BRIDGE.*

WE SHOULD STEP UP YOUR *SECURITY RATING* WITH IMMEDIATE EFFECT. AND PUT ALL AGENTS IN VENICE ON *IMMEDIATE ALERT.*

WE'D ALSO BETTER CONTACT AIRPORTS AND POINTS OF ENTRY INTO THE UK. I WANT ALEX RIDER BROUGHT IN.

UNHARMED, OF COURSE...?

WHATEVER IT TAKES.

SO TELL ME, ALEX, WHAT DO YOU *SEE?*

I SUPPOSE IT'S A MAN *FLYING* THROUGH THE SKY. HE'S WEARING A *BACKPACK.*

THAT'S EXCELLENT. VERY *GOOD!* REMEMBER, THE *RORSCHACH* TEST REQUIRES THAT YOU SAY THE FIRST THING YOU SEE. *DON'T* THINK TOO MUCH.

HOW ABOUT THIS ONE?

A *FOOTBALL*, BEING PUMPED UP.

I THOUGHT YOU WERE A *PSYCHIATRIST*.

I'M PERFECTLY *QUALIFIED* TO GIVE YOU AN INJECTION, ALEX.

DON'T TELL ME YOU'RE AFRAID OF A *LITTLE PRICK*?

THE REPORT ALSO SAYS YOU'RE A LITTLE *RUN-DOWN*. IT'S TO BE EXPECTED, AFTER ALL YOU'VE BEEN THROUGH, SO THE NURSE HAS SUGGESTED A *VITAMIN BOOSTER*.

WOULD YOU ROLL UP YOUR SLEEVE, PLEASE?

I WOULDN'T CALL YOU *THAT*...

VERY GOOD. OFF YOU GO! I AM SURE THERE ARE MORE TESTS FOR YOU TO UNDERGO BEFORE YOUR FINAL *REPORT* FROM MONSIEUR D'ARC.

THE BOY IS CERTAINLY *EXCEPTIONAL*, MRS ROTHMAN. HIS UNCLE TRAINED HIM ALMOST FROM BIRTH, AND DID A *VERY* GOOD JOB.

ALEX IS *INTELLIGENT*, *QUICK-WITTED*, AND EVERYONE HERE LIKES HIM. UNFORTUNATELY, I HAVE *DOUBTS* ABOUT HIS USEFULNESS TO US.

SUCH AS?

DESPITE HIS INEXPERIENCE, HE IS VERY GOOD ON THE *SHOOTING RANGE*. HE ALREADY HAS A *SEVENTY-TWO* PER CENT SCORE.

BUT TODAY, WHEN WE MADE HIM SHOOT *LIFELIKE* TARGETS, HIS SCORE DROPPED TO *FORTY-SIX* PER CENT.

GO ON.

HIS *RORSCHACH* TEST WAS ALSO TROUBLING. ONE SHAPE, WHICH EVERY STUDENT WE'VE HAD IDENTIFIES AS A MAN IN A *POOL OF BLOOD*, ALEX SAW A MAN WITH A JETPACK.

DESPITE YOUR PROGRESS, ALEX, YOU'RE *STILL* AFRAID OF KILLING. AND THAT MAKES YOU AFRAID OF SCORPIA. YOU HAVE TO GET OVER THAT.

SO HE *IS* GOING TO FAIL ME.

NO ... BUT YOU HAVE TO *TRUST* US A LITTLE MORE.

AFTER YOU'VE KILLED *ONCE*, YOU'LL SEE IT WASN'T *SUCH* A BIG DEAL. IT'S LIKE JUMPING INTO A SWIMMING POOL.

BUT YOU *HAVE* TO CROSS THAT PSYCHOLOGICAL BARRIER, IF YOU'RE TO BECOME ONE OF US.

I DON'T *WANT* TO CROSS IT. I'M *NOT* A KILLER.

SO YOU KEEP SAYING. BUT TOMORROW, D'ARC IS SENDING YOU TO ENGLAND, ON YOUR *FIRST MISSION* FOR SCORPIA.

WHY IS *ANYONE* TAKING THIS LETTER SERIOUSLY? WE GET *CRANK MAIL* ALL THE TIME.

BECAUSE, MR KELLNER, IT IS FROM *SCORPIA*. THE DUTY SERGEANT BROUGHT IT TO OUR ATTENTION AS SOON AS HE SAW THE *EMBOSSED SCORPION*. ALAS, THE MAN WHO DELIVERED IT WAS *LONG GONE*.

SO WE'RE DRAGGING THE *PRIME MINISTER* BACK FROM THE *MEXICO ENVIRONMENT SUMMIT* ... BECAUSE OF AN EMBOSSED SCORPION?

SIR GRAHAM, THIS IS *RIDICULOUS!*

HAVE YOU *READ* THE LETTER, MARK? THEY CLAIM TO HAVE INVENTED A NEW WEAPON THAT WILL KILL *THOUSANDS OF SCHOOL CHILDREN*. AND SCORPIA DO *NOT* MAKE IDLE THREATS.

BECAUSE THEY UNDERSTAND *POLITICS, MR KELLNER. IF AMERICA DOESN'T* AGREE TO SCORPIA'S DEMANDS, THE BRITISH PEOPLE WILL *NEVER* FORGIVE THEM.

THE *"SPECIAL RELATIONSHIP"* BETWEEN BRITAIN AND AMERICA WILL BE *DESTROYED* FOR EVER.

LOOK, I MAY ONLY BE THE PRIME MINISTER'S *SPECIAL ADVISOR*, BUT I KNOW A THING OR TWO ABOUT WEAPONS. YOU *CAN'T* MAKE ONE THAT WILL *ONLY* KILL CHILDREN ... OR *FOOTBALLERS*, LIKE THEY THREATEN!

I SPOKE TO *ALAN BLUNT* AT MI6 THIS AFTERNOON. THEY'RE *NOT* PREPARED TO RULE OUT THE POSSIBILITY THIS WEAPON EXISTS.

AND THE *"DEMONSTRATION"* MENTIONED IN THE LETTER, TO KILL THE *ENGLAND RESERVE FOOTBALL TEAM*, IS VERY WORRYING.

SCORPIA SAYS THEY WILL KILL THE TEAM AT *SEVEN-FIFTEEN*, AFTER THEY LAND AT HEATHROW AT FIVE PAST SEVEN. THAT'S MUCH *LATER* THAN SCHEDULED.

BUT *BRITISH AIRWAYS* TOLD ME THE FLIGHT WAS DELAYED IN *LAGOS*, AND WILL *INDEED* NOW LAND AT SEVEN OH FIVE.

WE MUST THEREFORE *RE-ROUTE* THE PLANE AT ONCE. IT CAN LAND AT BIRMINGHAM, OR MANCHESTER. WE *MUST* ENSURE THE PLAYERS' SAFETY.

I DON'T AGREE.

YOU MAY BE SCARED OF SCORPIA, BUT I THINK THEY'RE *IDIOTS*, AND WE SHOULD CALL THEIR BLUFF.

WE CAN USE THIS THREAT TO *TEST* THEIR "INVISIBLE SWORD". AND BY *SIXTEEN* MINUTES PAST SEVEN WE'LL KNOW IT DOESN'T EXIST!

YOU'RE WILLING TO *RISK* THE LIVES OF THE FOOTBALL PLAYERS?

THERE'S *NO* RISK! WE'LL THROW A MASSIVE *SECURITY BLANKET* AROUND HEATHROW, SO NOBODY CAN GET NEAR THEM. WE'LL HAVE A *HUNDRED* ARMED SOLDIERS SURROUNDING THE PLANE.

AND *HOW* WILL YOU GET A HUNDRED EXTRA ARMED GUARDS INTO HEATHROW? YOU'LL START A *PANIC*.

I'M A *SPIN DOCTOR*, SIR GRAHAM. I'VE HANDLED *WORSE* STORIES IN MY TIME.

WE'LL SAY IT'S A *TRAINING EXERCISE.*

LADIES AND GENTLEMEN, WELCOME TO *HEATHROW*.

FOR SOME REASON, THE CONTROL TOWER IS RE-ROUTING US *AWAY* FROM THE MAIN TERMINAL. NOTHING TO WORRY ABOUT, JUST SIT TIGHT...

HEATHROW AIRPOR

NOTHING TO *WORRY* ABOUT, EH? NOW, I MAY ONLY BE A *RESERVE* GOALIE...

...BUT AN ESCORT OF *ARMY JEEPS* IS THE SORT OF THING THAT *MAKES ME* WORRY!

THE *JEEPS* ARE WITH THE PLANE, AND *FOOT TROOPS* ARE IN POSITION. WE'VE GOT SNIPERS, DOGS, *EVERYTHING*. SO WHAT NOW?

NOW, WE WATCH EIGHTEEN PEOPLE *DIE*.

I **KNOW** KELLNER'S A BLOODY FOOL, BUT I ADMIT I CAN'T SEE **HOW** THEY'LL DO IT.

THE AIRPORT'S BEEN SEALED OFF FOR **HOURS**. WE'VE **TREBLED** SECURITY, AND EVERYONE IS ON **HIGH ALERT**. DID YOU CHECK THE PASSENGER LIST?

OF COURSE. TOURISTS, FAMILIES, BUSINESSMEN, TWO WEATHER FORECASTERS AND A TV CHEF. **NO** APPARENT THREAT AT ALL.

BUT SCORPIA **WILL** DO WHAT THEY SAY. THEY NEVER FAIL.

IT'S STILL POSSIBLE THEY MADE A MISTAKE **WARNING** US.

NO. THEY WARNED YOU BECAUSE THEY **KNEW** THERE WAS NOTHING YOU COULD DO. THEY **WANT** YOU TO SEE IT.

THIRTEEN MINUTES PAST. HERE WE GO.

...AND NOW YOU'VE INSTALLED A *METAL DETECTOR* IN RECEPTION, AND A *GUARD* OUTSIDE MY FRONT DOOR!

...I STILL DON'T THINK THIS IS *NECESSARY*, ALAN. THE BUILDING HAS *CAMERAS* EVERYWHERE, THE WALLS ARE TOO *SMOOTH* TO CLIMB...

FOR HEAVEN'S SAKE, THIS IS *ALEX RIDER* WE'RE TALKING ABOUT.

NO, MRS JONES ... THIS IS *SCORPIA* WE'RE TALKING ABOUT ...

GOOD NIGHT

BLUNT WANTS US TO LOOK OUT FOR A FOURTEEN-YEAR-OLD *KID*? WHAT HAPPENED, DID THEY FORGET HIS *BIRTHDAY*?

SEARCH ME.

HEY, DID YOU HEAR ABOUT THE *FOOTBALL TEAM*? SOME RARE *DISEASE* THEY GOT IN NIGERIA, APPARENTLY...

PROBABLY MALARIA. THEY'VE GOT THOSE GENETICALLY MODIFIED *SUPER-MOSQUITOES*, NOW...

HEY, *YOU!* WHO ARE YOU DELIVERING TO?

UH ... FOSTER. *PIZZA* FOR THE SIXTH FLOOR.

WE'RE GOING TO HAVE TO TAKE A *LOOK* IN THAT *BAG*.

WHATEVER, MAN, IT'S JUST A FRIGGIN' PIZZA AND A BOTTLE OF COKE.

IS THIS *FORT KNOX*, OR SOMETHIN'?

WHAT ARE THESE?

DRINKING STRAWS. WHAT'S IT *LOOK* LIKE?

AND THIS?

PROMOTION LEAFLET. YOU KNOW, PIZZA AND A DRINK FOR NINE NINETY-NINE. YOU WANNA *ORDER* ONE?

WATCH YOUR *LIP*, SUNSHINE.

...AND THE *FAKE* OLIVES IN THE *FAKE* PIZZA BOX. ALL TOO EASY.

...

MEEEOOOOW

SSSHHHH!

WHAT IS IT, *Q*? I ALREADY *FED* YOU, YOU GREEDY MOGGY. HONESTLY, YOUR APPETITE WILL BE THE—

STOP IT!

I KNOW YOU'RE JUST TRYING TO MAKE ME *HESITATE*. USING MY FIRST NAME, MAKING ME THINK OF YOU AS A *PERSON* INSTEAD OF A *TARGET*...

JUST TELL ME *WHY* YOU DID IT!

WHY DID YOU KILL MY FATHER?!

WHY DO YOU *CARE*, ALEX? YOU NEVER *KNEW* JOHN RIDER. YOU HAVE *NO* MEMORY OF HIM. DO YOU KNOW HOW MANY PEOPLE HE *MURDERED*?

AND NOW SCORPIA WANT *YOU* TO FOLLOW IN HIS FOOTSTEPS.

YOU *CHEATED!* YOU SAID YOU WOULD LET HIM GO, BUT I *SAW* THE VIDEO! *YOU* GAVE THE ORDER, AND *SHOT* HIM IN THE BACK!

I *COULDN'T* LET YOUR FATHER GO BACK TO SCORPIA, ALEX. IT WAS *TOO DANGEROUS*.

BUT I DON'T THINK *YOU'RE* A KILLER. YOU HAVE A CHOICE...

TWO AGENTS BROUGHT ME IN THROUGH *HEATHROW*, DISGUISED AS AN *ITALIAN* FAMILY. I DON'T KNOW THEIR NAMES.

THEY HAD A *LAYOUT* OF MRS JONES' FLAT. EVERYTHING EXCEPT FOR THAT *GLASS SCREEN*. ALL I HAD TO DO WAS WAIT FOR HER.

THEY GAVE ME A *NUMBER* TO CALL WHEN I'D KILLED HER. BUT THEY'LL KNOW *YOU'VE* GOT ME, NOW.

WHERE *IS* MRS JONES?

SHE DIDN'T WANT TO SEE YOU.

ALEX ... YOU'VE BEEN *MORE* USEFUL TO US THAN I COULD POSSIBLY HAVE CALCULATED.

BUT IN TRUTH, I WISH WE HAD NEVER MET, BECAUSE YOU DON'T BELONG IN MY WORLD ANY MORE THAN *I* BELONG IN YOURS.

UNFORTUNATELY, I *CAN'T* LET YOU GO BACK TO SCHOOL...

I JUST WANT TO GO BACK TO SCHOOL. I DON'T WANT TO SEE *ANY* OF YOU, *EVER* AGAIN. NOT YOU, NOT SCORPIA ... YOU CAN *ALL* GO TO *HELL*!

...BECAUSE IN THIRTY HOURS EVERY CHILD THERE COULD BE *DEAD.*

ALONG WITH *THOUSANDS MORE* CHILDREN IN LONDON.

THAT IS WHAT YOUR *"FRIENDS"* IN SCORPIA HAVE PROMISED. THEY HAVE MADE DEMANDS WE *CANNOT* MEET, AND I HAVE NO DOUBT THEY *WILL* CARRY OUT THEIR THREAT TO MAKE US PAY A HEAVY PRICE.

AS TO HOW... WE DON'T KNOW. BUT *YOU* MIGHT.

THOUSANDS...? WHAT ARE YOU TALKING ABOUT? *HOW?*

ASSASSINATION...

THE *A* IN *SCORPIA,* YES. THIS IS NO IDLE THREAT.

BUT THEY MADE A MISTAKE. THEY SENT YOU TO *US.*

THAT'S NOT *QUITE* WHAT THEY SAID. AND THEY'VE OFFERED *TWO HUNDRED FBI AGENTS* TO HELP US TRACK SCORPIA DOWN.

FOREIGN SECRETARY

BUT THE *PRESIDENT* HAS A POINT. THESE DEMANDS ARE *IMPOSSIBLE*, AND THE LETTER CLEARLY SAYS THEY WILL *NOT* NEGOTIATE.

THEY COULD STILL *TRY!*

ARGUING WILL GET US *NOWHERE*. DOCTOR, YOU SAID YOU HAD THE REPORT ON THE *FOOTBALLERS*...?

THEY WERE ALL *POISONED*. WE FOUND TRACES OF *CYANIDE*, DELIVERED STRAIGHT TO THE HEART. SMALL AMOUNTS, BUT ENOUGH TO *KILL*.

WE DON'T KNOW HOW. THEY HADN'T BEEN *SHOT*, AND THERE WERE *NO* PERFORATIONS ON THE SKIN. THE ONLY ODD THING IN THEIR BLOOD WAS TINY TRACES OF *GOLD*.

GOLD? DID *THAT* CONTRIBUTE TO THEIR DEATH?

WE, AH, WE DON'T *THINK* SO. BUT EVERY ONE OF THE PLAYERS WAS THE SAME...

THIS ALL SEEMS PRETTY *OBVIOUS* TO ME. THE *ONLY* TIME THEY COULD HAVE BEEN POISONED SIMULTANEOUSLY IS WHEN THEY WERE SERVED *FOOD* ON THE PLANE.

BUT IF THERE'S *NO* SECRET WEAPON, WHAT'S *"INVISIBLE SWORD"*?

IT'S A *TRICK!* THEY'RE TRYING TO MAKE US THINK THEY CAN KILL PEOPLE BY *REMOTE CONTROL!*

REMOTE CONTROL ... WHAT DOES THAT REMIND ME OF?

EVEN IF THEY *WERE* ALL POISONED AT THE SAME TIME, A PERSON'S METABOLISM IS *UNIQUE.* THE CYANIDE WOULD HAVE ACTED AT DIFFERENT SPEEDS ON EACH OF THEM.

THEY WERE ALL *ATHLETES!* NOT VERY GOOD ATHLETES, BUT STILL ... THEIR METABOLISMS WOULD BE SIMILAR ENOUGH. THE WHOLE THING IS A *BLUFF!*

THAT ISN'T *NORMALLY* SCORPIA'S WAY.

WE'VE DEALT WITH THEM BEFORE, AND THEY'VE *NEVER* YET MADE A HOLLOW THREAT.

YOU WERE *AT* HEATHROW, ALAN. WHAT DO *YOU* THINK HAPPENED?

I DON'T KNOW.

WELL, THAT'S *VERY* HELPFUL, ISN'T IT? SO MUCH FOR THE *"INTELLIGENCE"* SERVICES!

COULD YOU AT LEAST TELL US WHY YOU'VE BROUGHT YOUR *SON* ALONG?

THIS IS ALEX RIDER. AS YOU ALL KNOW, ALEX HAS HELPED US ON A NUMBER OF PAST OCCASIONS.

HE IS ALSO THE LAST PERSON HERE TO HAVE HAD *CONTACT* WITH SCORPIA.

YEAH, I JOINED—

I SENT ALEX TO *INFILTRATE* SCORPIA, UNDERCOVER, IN *MALAGOSTO*. WE NEEDED TO KNOW CERTAIN DETAILS ABOUT THEIR TRAINING GROUNDS.

WOW. BLUNT *LIED* TO PROTECT ME ... AND YOU'D NEVER KNOW. LYING COMES *EASILY* TO HIM.

IF WE *KNOW* WHERE SCORPIA ARE, WHY DON'T WE SEND IN THE *SAS* AND KILL THE LOT OF THEM?

POLICE COMMISSIONE

THE *ITALIAN GOVERNMENT* WOULD NOT TAKE KINDLY TO HAVING THEIR TERRITORY *INVADED*, COMMISSIONER.

BESIDES, SCORPIA IS A *GLOBAL* OPERATION, AND WE DON'T KNOW ALL THE LEADERS. THEY WOULD COME FOR *REVENGE*.

ALAN BLUNT

AND WHAT DID THE FAMOUS ALEX RIDER *FIND* AT MALAGOSTO?

MRS ROTHMAN MENTIONED *INVISIBLE SWORD*, AND...

SOMETHING ABOUT A *"COLD CHAIN"*? I DON'T KNOW IF THAT'S CONNECTED.

WE'RE WASTING TIME. THE FOOTBALLERS WERE ALL TOGETHER, SO IT WAS *EASY* TO POISON THEM IN THE SAME PLACE.

BUT HOW WOULD YOU DO THAT WITH *THOUSANDS* OF SCHOOLKIDS?!

SCHOOL ... OF COURSE!

INJECTIONS!

EVERY CHILD GETS INJECTED FOR *VACCINATIONS* AT THE START OF TERM. AT *CONSANTO*, I SAW TEST TUBES CONTAINING LIQUID ... AND LOADS OF TRAYS, WITH WHAT LOOKED LIKE *EGGS*.

SOME VACCINES ARE *GROWN* IN EGGS. CONSANTO SUPPLY VACCINES ALL OVER THE WORLD ...

AND THAT *ALSO* EXPLAINS THE "COLD CHAIN". VACCINES MUST BE KEPT AT A *CONSTANT TEMPERATURE* DURING TRANSPORTATION. BREAK THE CHAIN, AND THE VACCINE IS *RUINED*.

YOU MENTIONED "REMOTE CONTROL". WELL, MRS ROTHMAN KEPT A *SIBERIAN TIGER* IN HER VENICE OFFICE.

OH, FOR— YOU EXPECT US TO *BELIEVE* THIS RUBBISH?

IT ATTACKED ME, BUT THEN SOMEONE PRESSED A BUTTON ON WHAT LOOKED LIKE A *TV REMOTE*...

... AND THE TIGER JUST LAY DOWN AND *SLEPT*.

NANOSHELLS.

"NANOSHELLS"? SOUNDS LIKE SOMETHING OUT OF *SCIENCE FICTION!* WHO ARE YOU, ANYWAY?

DR *RACHEL STEPHENSON.* I'M A WRITER AND RESEARCHER IN *NANOTECH,* AND IT'S FAR FROM FICTION.

IT'S ALREADY BEING USED AND RESEARCHED BY FOOD COMPANIES, DRUG AGENCIES, AND THE MILITARY.

I THINK IT'S ALSO BEING USED HERE. THE *GOLD PARTICLES* GOT ME THINKING, AND NOW ALEX HAS MADE IT *CLEAR.*

SCORPIA INJECTED THE FOOTBALLERS, AND THE CHILDREN, WITH *GOLD-COATED NANOSHELLS.*

IMAGINE A *TINY BULLET*, A THOUSAND TIMES THINNER THAN A HUMAN HAIR. THE INSIDE WOULD BE A POLYMER COMPOUND, WITH *CYANIDE* MIXED IN.

THE OUTER SHELL IS SOLID GOLD. THEN YOU FIX A *PROTEIN* TO THE OUTSIDE.

THE PROTEIN *GUIDES* THE BULLET, LIKE A HEAT-SEEKING MISSILE, TO THE *HEART*. AND IT STAYS THERE.

YOU WOULDN'T NEED TO INJECT MANY, AND THEY'D BE *INVISIBLE* TO THE NAKED EYE ... EVEN TO MOST *MICROSCOPES*.

BUT YOU SAID THE POISON IS SAFE, *PROTECTED* BY THE GOLD.

YES, SIR. IF YOU LEAVE IT ALONE, IT'LL JUST *PASS OUT* OF THE BODY AFTER A WHILE, AND NOBODY WOULD KNOW.

BUT SCORPIA COULD *BREAK UP* THE GOLD, LIKE ALEX SAID, BY REMOTE CONTROL.

HAVE YOU EVER PUT AN EGG IN A MICROWAVE? THE SHELL *EXPLODES*. SO THEY COULD BE PLANNING TO USE *MICROWAVE* TECHNOLOGY.

NO, MICROWAVES WOULD BE TOO LOW FREQUENCY. I'M NO EXPERT ON *PLASMON RESONANCE*...

A *TERAHERTZ BEAM* MIGHT DO IT.

THIS IS ALL *WAY* OVER MY HEAD.

TERAHERTZ BEAMS ARE BEING DEVELOPED FOR MEDICAL IMAGING, AND SATELLITE COMMUNICATIONS.

THEY CAN DO THIS FROM A SATELLITE, IN *SPACE*?

...MY GOD.

ACTUALLY, *NO*. THE BEAM WOULD BE TOO WEAK. I THINK THEY ERECTED A *SATELLITE DISH* SOMEWHERE CLOSE TO HEATHROW, WHEN THOSE FOOTBALLERS LANDED.

SO ALL THEY HAD TO DO WAS FLICK A SWITCH, AND *BOOM*. THE BEAMS BROKE DOWN THE GOLD, AND *RELEASED* THE CYANIDE.

WE'RE LOOKING FOR A **SAUCER**, LIKE A BIG SATELLITE TV DISH. PROBABLY MOUNTED ON THE SIDE OF AN OFFICE BUILDING, BECAUSE IT WOULD NEED **LINE OF SIGHT** TO WORK.

SIR ... YOU **MUST** EVACUATE LONDON.

THE LETTER STATES THE CHILDREN WILL DIE AT FOUR O'CLOCK **TOMORROW**. WE DON'T KNOW HOW **FAR** THESE BEAMS CAN REACH. THERE MAY BE SEVERAL DISHES, MOUNTED ON BUILDINGS **THROUGHOUT** THE CITY.

AN EVACUATION OF THAT SCALE, BY TOMORROW AFTERNOON? IT'S **IMPOSSIBLE**! AND WHAT WOULD WE **TELL** PEOPLE?

THE TRUTH.

ABSOLUTELY **NOT**. YOU'D START A MASS PANIC THAT WOULD BECOME A **STAMPEDE**.

BESIDES, IF THE PM GOES ON **TV** AND **ANNOUNCES** WE'RE EVACUATING, WHAT'S TO STOP SCORPIA FLICKING THE SWITCH **EARLY**?

I *AGREE* WITH MARK. WE NOW *KNOW* WHAT INVISIBLE SWORD IS, AND THAT'S OUR *ONLY* ADVANTAGE. WE CAN'T RISK LOSING IT.

DOCTOR, WOULD WE *RECOGNIZE* THESE DISHES IF WE SAW THEM?

I THINK SO, YES. THEY'D BE QUITE BIG, AND AT LEAST A *HUNDRED METRES* UP.

AND *NOT* AUTHORIZED TO BE MOUNTED THERE.

WE'LL NEED A LIST OF EVERY CHILD WHO *RECEIVED* A VACCINE DEVELOPED BY CONSANTO. THAT MAY GIVE US A CLUE TO WHICH *AREAS* OF LONDON TO CHECK FIRST.

THIS IS *JUST* AS IMPOSSIBLE AS EVACUATING. WE DON'T EVEN KNOW HOW MANY WE'RE LOOKING FOR.

IF EVEN *ONE* DISH REMAINS UNDETECTED, CHILDREN WILL *STILL* DIE.

TEETH BRACES?!

ACTUALLY, IT'S A LOOPED *RADIO AERIAL*, MADE ENTIRELY OF TRANSPARENT PLASTIC.

I FEEL *TERRIBLE* SENDING YOU IN WITH NO WEAPONS. I'VE BEEN WORKING ON A RUBIK'S CUBE *HAND GRENADE*, AND SOME ROLLERBLADES THAT ARE *REAL* BLADES...

YOU ACTIVATE THIS TINY, HIDDEN *SWITCH* WITH YOUR *TONGUE*.

IT SENDS A *DISTRESS SIGNAL*, SO WE CAN COME RUSHING IN!

THAT WILL BE ALL, SMITHERS.

AS SOON AS YOU FIND THE *DISHES*, OR IF YOU JUST FEEL YOU'RE IN ANY *DANGER* AT ALL, ACTIVATE THE SWITCH. WE'LL SEND SPECIAL FORCES IN TO PULL YOU OUT.

ALL RIGHT. NOW ... HOW WILL YOU MAKE SCORPIA BELIEVE I *ESCAPED*?

...WORST **TRAFFIC ACCIDENT** IN RECENT YEARS, INVOLVING AT LEAST A **DOZEN** VEHICLES. PARAMEDICS SAY IT WAS A **MIRACLE** NOBODY WAS KILLED, ALTHOUGH MANY WERE **INJURED**...

...WITNESSES SAY A **TEENAGE BOY** TRAVELLING IN THE FIRST CAR **FLED** THE SCENE, PURSUED BY A **MAN** IN A DARK SUIT AND SUNGLASSES. NEITHER HAS YET BEEN **LOCATED**...

THIS IS **ALEX RIDER**. I NEED TO TALK TO **NILE**.

FIRST TELL US WHAT HAPPENED. IS THE WOMAN **DEAD**?

YES, BUT THEY **CAUGHT** ME ON THE WAY OUT. THEY WERE **TAKING** ME SOMEWHERE THIS AFTERNOON, AND I MANAGED TO **ESCAPE**.

LOOK, YOU SAID YOU'D BRING ME **IN** WHEN I'D DONE IT. I'M IN A PHONE BOX, **EVERYONE'S** LOOKING FOR ME...

ONE EACH SIDE, FACING *NORTH*, *SOUTH* AND *EAST*. AND THEY'RE ALL LINKED UP TO THIS...

...A *TRANSMITTER*, PROGRAMMED TO BEGIN EMITTING HIGH FREQUENCY *TERAHERTZ BEAMS* AT FOUR O'CLOCK THIS AFTERNOON.

10 DOWNING STREET

FANTASTIC NEWS ... YES, OF *COURSE* I WANT YOU TO DISCONNECT THEM! *RIGHT NOW!*

GENTLEMEN, WE'VE *DONE* IT. NATURALLY WE'LL KEEP LOOKING, IN CASE SCORPIA HAD A BACK-UP. BUT WE'LL FIND *THEM*, TOO.

THE CRISIS IS *OVER.*

WHAT DO *YOU* THINK? IS THAT REALLY IT?

LIVERPOOL STREET

SCORPIA ARE MORE *CLEVER* THAN THAT. IF THESE DISHES HAVE BEEN FOUND, IT'S ONLY BECAUSE THEY WERE *MEANT* TO BE FOUND.

SO KELLNER IS WRONG AGAIN.

THE MAN'S A BLOODY *FOOL*.

WE DON'T HAVE MUCH TIME.

NO. ALL WE HAVE IS *ALEX RIDER*.

ALEX! SORRY WE'RE RUNNING LATE, MY DEAR, BUT IT'S RATHER A BUSY DAY.

NOW, I WANT YOU TO SEE THE FRUITS OF DR LIEBERMANN'S *HANDIWORK*...

THE *SCORPIA AGENT* WHO PICKED ME UP LAST NIGHT *DUMPED* ME IN HERE ... AND NOTHING SINCE!

...BUT FIRST, WE'RE GOING TO HAVE TO *SEARCH* YOU. I'LL WAIT DOWNSTAIRS WHILE NILE CHECKS YOU OVER.

IS THIS *IT*? ARE THEY JUST GOING TO LEAVE ME HERE, AND WATCH ME *DIE* WHEN THE NANOSHELLS EXPLODE AT FOUR O'CLOCK?

IT'S NOT THAT WE DON'T TRUST YOU. BUT SCORPIA TAKES *NO* CHANCES, AND IT'S POSSIBLE MI6 *CONTAMINATED* YOU OR SOMETHING WHILE YOU WERE THEIR PRISONER.

TAKE YOUR CLOTHES OFF.

SCORPIA BOUGHT IT A COUPLE OF YEARS AGO. WE'VE MADE ONE OR TWO *ADJUSTMENTS*, OF COURSE.

LIGHTS!

WELCOME, ALEX...

TO *INVISIBLE SWORD!*

THIS IS THE *NERVE CENTRE* OF THE WHOLE MAD OPERATION! ARMED GUARDS EVERYWHERE, AND *PROOF* THAT MARK KELLNER WAS WRONG. SCORPIA *ISN'T* USING DISHES ON A BUILDING...

...THEY'VE ATTACHED THEM TO A *HOT-AIR BALLOON!*

WHAT DO YOU THINK, ALEX? *IMPRESSIVE*, NO?

I DON'T KNOW HOW THEY'RE GOING TO GET THAT BALLOON OUT OF HERE, BUT THIS MUST BE IT! I'VE GOT TO BUY SOME TIME...

ARE YOU GOING FOR A BALLOON RIDE? HOW WILL YOU GET IT OUT OF THE CHURCH?

I'M NOT GOING ANYWHERE. LET ME EXPLAIN.

I REPEAT, THE DISHES ARE ON A *HOT-AIR BALLOON!* WE NEED STINGER MISSILES TO BRING IT DOWN!

NEGATIVE, COMMANDER. THIS IS *LONDON*, NOT *BAGHDAD.* SHOOT IT DOWN!

OUR RIFLES DON'T HAVE THE *RANGE!*

KRAK

YOU'LL HAVE TO CALL IN AN *AIR STRIKE!* CONDITION RED!

AN AIR STRIKE...?

DO IT. OF COURSE, THAT'S ASSUMING THEY CAN GET THERE IN *TIME*.

OTHERWISE, IT'S ALL DOWN TO ALEX.

SO, ALEX. IT'S BEEN A WEEK, HAVE YOU SETTLED BACK DOWN INTO NORMAL LIFE?

MORE OR LESS. I TOLD MY TEACHERS I GOT *MUGGED*.

JACK STARBRIGHT THINKS I'M *MENTAL* FOR EVEN COMING BACK HERE.

ALAN BLUNT'S OFFICE, MI6 HEADQUARTERS

YES, WELL, I ASKED YOU IN TO GIVE YOU AN *UPDATE*.

SCORPIA'S PLOT WAS A COMPLETE *FAILURE*, AND I DOUBT THEY'LL TRY ANYTHING LIKE IT AGAIN. YOU DID A VERY GOOD JOB.

THEY ALSO LOST ONE OF THEIR TOP ASSASSINS, THAT MAN *NILE*. WHAT HAPPENED TO HIM?

I THINK HE JUST GOT TIRED ... BURNED OUT.

OH! YOU WERE THE BOY SCORPIA *KIDNAPPED.*

THE CIVIL SERVANT'S *SON*, ON ALBERT BRIDGE!

THAT'S RIGHT.

I WAS *EIGHTEEN* AT THE TIME, AND SCORPIA THOUGHT KIDNAPPING ME COULD FORCE MY FATHER TO *CHANGE* GOVERNMENT POLICY.

BUT THAT'S *NOT* HOW GOVERNMENT WORKS. THERE WAS NOTHING HE COULD DO. SCORPIA TOLD ME I WAS GOING TO DIE...

UNTIL MI6 OFFERED THEM AN *EXCHANGE*.

FRANKLY, I THOUGHT THEY MIGHT JUST DUMP ME IN THE *THAMES* ON THE WAY TO THE BRIDGE. THAT BITCH JULIA ROTHMAN CERTAINLY WANTED TO.

"ANYWAY, YOUR FATHER AND I SET OFF ACROSS THE BRIDGE, AS YOU KNOW. AND WHEN WE PASSED IN THE MIDDLE, HE *SPOKE* TO ME.

"HE SAID, "*THERE'S GOING TO BE SHOOTING. RUN AS FAST AS YOU CAN, AND DON'T LOOK BACK.*"

"SO I DID, OF COURSE, EVEN THOUGH I WAS *TERRIFIED* WHEN I SAW YOUR FATHER GET *SHOT*. I REACHED MI6, AND THEY BUNDLED ME OFF IN A CAR."

SO MY FATHER ... *SACRIFICED* HIMSELF FOR YOU. EVEN THOUGH HE'D *NEVER* MET YOU.

YES, BUT THAT WASN'T THE END OF IT. ERM...?

GO ON, JAMES. IT'S ALL RIGHT.

SHE PLANTED A **BOMB** ON THE PLANE. YOUR PARENTS DIED TOGETHER, WHICH I SUPPOSE IS A SMALL MERCY.

ALEX? ARE YOU ALL RIGHT?

WHY DIDN'T YOU **TELL** ME? I ALMOST KILLED YOU, YOU SENT ME BACK TO SCORPIA WITH **MRS ROTHMAN**, YOU...

WHY DIDN'T YOU TELL ME THIS BEFORE?

BECAUSE THAT WOULD HAVE BEEN **MANIPULATIVE**. OF COURSE YOU WOULD HAVE WANTED REVENGE.

BUT WE WANTED YOU TO GO BACK TO SCORPIA FOR THE **SAME** REASONS YOUR FATHER WENT TO ALBERT BRIDGE... AS A CHOICE, BECAUSE YOU KNEW IT WAS THE **RIGHT THING** TO DO.